Brenda and Edward

To Genevieve, Joanna and Gregory Sheppard, and Max

First U.S. edition 1997 published by
Kids Can Press Ltd.
85 River Rock Drive, Suite 202
Buffalo, NY 14207

Published in Canada by
Kids Can Press Ltd.
29 Birch Avenue
Toronto, ON M4V 1E2

Designed by Wycliffe Smith
Printed in Hong Kong by Everbest Printing Co., Ltd.

84 0 9 8 7 6 5 4 3

Canadian Cataloguing in Publication Data
Kovalski, Maryann
Brenda and Edward

ISBN 0-919964-77-X

I. Title.

PS8571.092B73 1984 jC813'.54 C84-098730-7
PZ10.3.K68Br 1984

Brenda and Edward

Maryann Kovalski

KIDS CAN PRESS LTD.

Brenda and Edward were two happy dogs.
They lived behind a French restaurant in a large
cardboard box which they had made very cozy.

In winter they would sit by the fire
and Edward would read aloud.

In summer they would sit on
Mrs. Levitt's steps and watch people.

Edward worked as a night watchdog
in a garage on the other side of town.
He left for work every afternoon at
four o'clock.

One day Edward was late, so he
left in a hurry and forgot his dinner.

Brenda ran after him calling his name, but
the street was noisy and he could not hear her.

She thought she saw him
going down the subway stairs.

Pushing her way through the crowd, she ran
down the steps, under the turnstile, and onto
the train.

The doors slammed shut, the train jerked,
and Brenda could hardly stand up. Her heart
pounded so loudly she couldn't hear all the
people laughing at her.

"A dog on the subway!" a lady laughed.
"Did you pay your fare?"

The moment the train stopped, Brenda
raced out the doors and ran up the stairs.

"I'll just go home and wait for Edward," she said to herself. That thought made her feel much better.

But when she reached the street, she
did not know where she was. It was
dark and nothing looked familiar.

Brenda thought she saw Edward going
into a drugstore across the street. She ran
to him without looking left or right.

A car screeched. Brenda saw the lights and heard a thud. She rolled over and over.

Then she lay very still and looked up at all the faces bent over her.

"The dog's just had a nasty fright," said a man. "It's only a filthy stray," said another. "Take her to the pound and let them take care of her."

But the lady who drove the car stroked
Brenda's head and spoke softly in her ear.

Two men lifted Brenda into the back of the car. The door slammed shut and the car disappeared into the night.

The next morning, Edward returned from work to
find an empty house.
"Hmmm, that's strange," he muttered.
He was hungry, but he settled into his chair to read
the paper and wait for Brenda. He waited and waited.

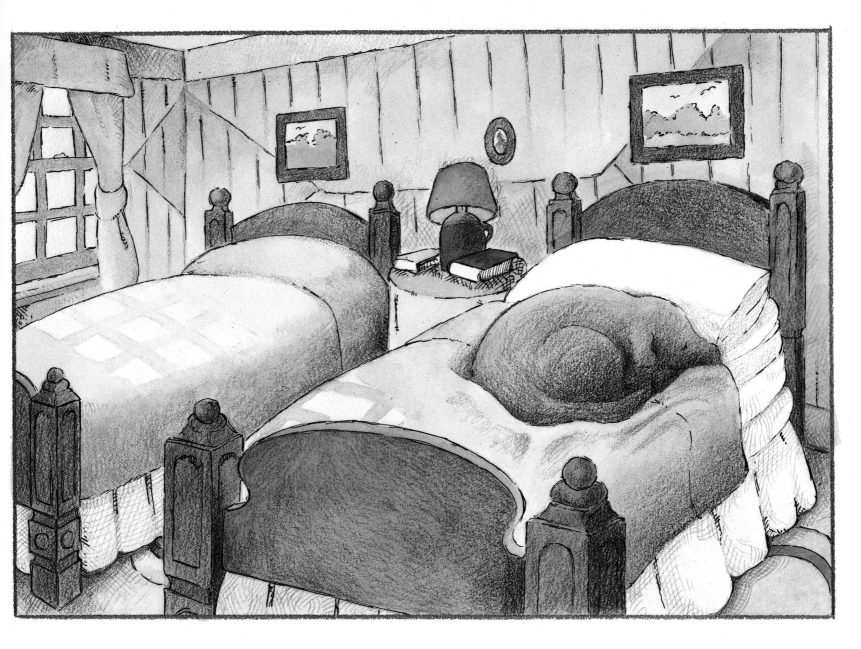

After a while, Edward became a little worried.
"I'm sure something has happened to her,"
he said very softly.
He crawled onto his bed to think.
He wasn't hungry anymore.

Finally Edward decided to get up and search for
Brenda. He sniffed everywhere in the neighborhood.
He even went to other neighborhoods far away.
He sniffed and he sniffed, but he never found her.

Many years passed and Edward became an old dog.
The man at the garage began to talk of replacing him
with a younger dog. This made Edward sad, but the
saddest thing in his whole life had already happened
when he lost Brenda, so he only sighed.

On the morning of his last day at work, he was
gathering his things. Suddenly he heard a lady shouting
at the owner of the garage.
"You call this fixed? I should call the police!"
Edward looked up at the angriest customer he had ever seen.

As the lady got ready to leave, Edward walked up
to the car and sniffed the tires, just out of habit.
When she opened the door, Edward stopped.
A smell came from the car that could belong to
only one dog — Brenda. Edward jumped into
the car and nothing anyone tried could make
him leave.

Finally the lady decided to take Edward home
with her. They drove for a long, long time.
They drove all the way to the country.

As the sun was setting, they reached the grandest house
Edward had ever seen. And there on the front porch was
Brenda — a little older, of course, but still a handsome dog.

After a touching reunion, Brenda and Edward
had dinner and watched the moon rise over the hills.

And after that they lived happily ever after,
two happy dogs once more.